MORTALS & IMMORTALS
of greek mythology

Françoise Rachmuhl ❊ Charlotte Gastaut

For Prudence and Violette,
My know-it-alls.
&
For Albert,
My I-don't-know-what.
C. G.

ROAR™

Fountaindale Public Library
Bolingbrook, IL
(630) 759-2102

In the Beginning

In the beginning of the world, there was Chaos, a dark abyss, formless, and without end. Then the Earth Mother, Gaia, appeared. And from her came the forests, mountains, the waves of the sea, animals, and Uranus, the starry sky.

Together with Gaia, Uranus gave birth to all sorts of beings. Some were monstrous, like the Hundred-Handed Ones, with their prodigious strength, and the Cyclopes, built as tall as towers with a single eye in the middle of their foreheads. These dangerous creatures were exiled to the bottom of the abyss—the Underworld.

Gaia also gave birth to the giants, the Titans, and their sisters, the Titanesses. But they all stayed stuck in her bosom, because Uranus lay on her and prevented her children from coming to light.

The last born, Chronos, revolted. His mother made him a small scythe with which he managed to injure his father. Uranus ran away and settled at the top of the world. From that point, the sky and the ground were separated, and day and night followed each other. Chronos took power and married his sister, Rhea, a Titaness.

The gods are their children and their grandchildren. They feed on nectar and ambrosia, which renders them immortal. Twelve among them are considered the most important. Because they live on Mount Olympus—a tall mountain in the north of Greece—we call them Olympians. In this book you will find their story.

Born from the
sea-foam

APHRODITE

CHAOS

URANUS GAIA

THE TITANS THE TITANESSES THE CYCLOPES THE HUNDRED-HANDED ONES

CHRONOS RHEA

HESTIA

DEMETER

HERA

HADES

POSEIDON

ZEUS

with **Metis**

with **Maia**

with **Leto**

with **Semele**

ARES

ATHENA

HERMES

HEPHAESTUS

APOLLO

ARTEMIS

DIONYSUS

ZEUS
The King of the Gods and the Master of the World

Jupiter in Latin. The son of Chronos and Rhea. The sky is his kingdom. He wields lightning and the oak is his sacred symbol. The eagle is his favorite animal. He looks like an adult in his prime, sporting a beard, and, most often, is shirtless. Zeus is the most powerful of the gods, but he wasn't always. Before he came to power, he had to overcome many trials.

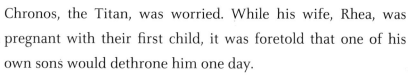

Chronos, the Titan, was worried. While his wife, Rhea, was pregnant with their first child, it was foretold that one of his own sons would dethrone him one day.

Chronos was big and tall, with a strong appetite and a large stomach. When the child was born, he made his decision. Under the pretext of admiring him more closely, he brought the child to his face, and then opened his mouth and swallowed him. He did the same with the four following children.

Rhea was in despair. When she was pregnant again, she confided in her mother, Gaia, who consoled her and gave her some advice.

When it was time for her to give birth, Rhea snuck out of her palace and went to Crete. She climbed a mountain, found a cave, and made herself at home. There, she gave birth to a large boy whom she named Zeus. She swaddled him in the golden cradle she had made sure to bring with her.

But she couldn't stay long. She had to make sure Chronos didn't notice her absence. Who would be able to take care of the baby? Who would feed him?

That was when she noticed two young girls in the cave. They were two nymphs, graceful divinities in charge of watching over the waters, mountains, and forests. In front of them stood a large goat, with long hair and golden horns. She approached the goat's udder, and Zeus began to suck.

"This is Amalthea, the goat," said the nymphs. "She will give her milk to your child. When he is a little older, he'll also be able to eat honey. There are plenty of bees on the top of the mountain."

"Thank you, thank you. However...what will happen if he makes any noise? Babies babble, cry, and laugh...his father might hear. Chronos has great hearing."

"Then we will call the Korybantes, the young warriors in charge of defending the country. When they hit their shields and swords together while stomping their feet and singing hymns, they will drown out any sound."

Rhea thanked the nymphs and then bent over to kiss her son one last time. Zeus was already asleep. He looked happy, smiling with a drop of milk at the corner of his upturned mouth. The Titaness left, reassured. But she still had more to do.

When she returned to the palace, she slipped into her chambers and began to moan, as if she was giving birth. Finally, she called her husband.

"Where is he? Where's the newborn?" he asked. "Give him to me!"

Rhea handed him a large rock wrapped in a blanket and, without delay, Chronos swallowed it. The rock passed easily from his throat to his stomach.

Years passed, and Zeus grew up. He had left the cave and was now living in the mountain among the shepherds. He partook in their games and festivals and, like them, took care of the goats. Sometimes, he would descend the mountain to the edge of the water. He knew that beyond the water, further on land, was his father's palace.

One night, he was walking along the beach when he noticed a beautiful young woman smiling at him as she stepped out from the waves. He rubbed his eyes, and in the next moment, he could no longer see her. Instead, all he saw was a white seagull floating above the waves. Was he dreaming? And now instead of the bird, a prancing dolphin. But he barely had time to reach out to pet the dolphin when a mocking laugh sounded out, and the young woman reappeared.

"Who are you?" asked Zeus. "Are you a magician?"

"I am an Oceanid, and I like to transform. My name is Metis, which means both wisdom and cunning. I know who you are and that you wish to free your siblings, trapped in Chronos's stomach. Find your mother and ask her to find a potion that will make someone throw up. You will present yourself to him as a cupbearer; serve him a drink, and you'll put the honey potion in the brew that you'll offer to your father. Then you'll see what will happen...go!

Following Metis's advice, Zeus introduced himself as a cupbearer. Ever the glutton, Chronos ate and drank an enormous amount over the course of the meal and soon took to vomiting. He first vomited the large rock he had swallowed in place of Zeus. And then, one after the other, his five first children in the inverse order of their birth: Poseidon, Hades, Hera, Demeter, and Hestia. The two gods and three goddesses took a stand behind Zeus.

"You are still young," they told him, "but you proved your intelligence and courage. Be our leader."

Zeus accepted and led his brothers and sisters to the top of Olympus, the tall mountain crowned with snow and bathed in light. It became the residence of the gods, and they became known as Olympians.

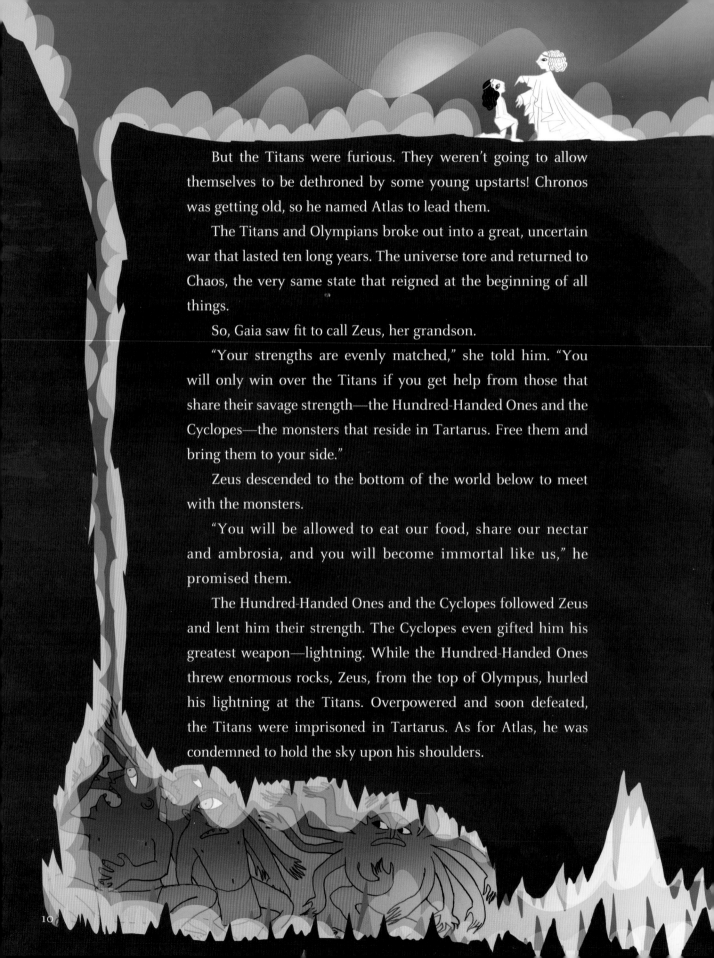

But the Titans were furious. They weren't going to allow themselves to be dethroned by some young upstarts! Chronos was getting old, so he named Atlas to lead them.

The Titans and Olympians broke out into a great, uncertain war that lasted ten long years. The universe tore and returned to Chaos, the very same state that reigned at the beginning of all things.

So, Gaia saw fit to call Zeus, her grandson.

"Your strengths are evenly matched," she told him. "You will only win over the Titans if you get help from those that share their savage strength—the Hundred-Handed Ones and the Cyclopes—the monsters that reside in Tartarus. Free them and bring them to your side."

Zeus descended to the bottom of the world below to meet with the monsters.

"You will be allowed to eat our food, share our nectar and ambrosia, and you will become immortal like us," he promised them.

The Hundred-Handed Ones and the Cyclopes followed Zeus and lent him their strength. The Cyclopes even gifted him his greatest weapon—lightning. While the Hundred-Handed Ones threw enormous rocks, Zeus, from the top of Olympus, hurled his lightning at the Titans. Overpowered and soon defeated, the Titans were imprisoned in Tartarus. As for Atlas, he was condemned to hold the sky upon his shoulders.

The Olympians rewarded Zeus, who led them to victory, with power. He became the king of the gods and master of the world, who would reign over justice and order. He divided the universe into three kingdoms that he shared with his two brothers after they pulled lots. Zeus received the sky, Poseidon the oceans, and Hades the Underworld. The Earth itself belonged to the three of them, together.

To ensure his reign would last and be peaceful, Zeus decided to marry. His first wife was Metis; his second was his sister, Hera. But Zeus had innumerable adventures and many children—gods when their mother was a goddess, and demigods when she was but a mortal. And many of these gods found their place among the Olympians.

HERA
Goddess of Marriage

Juno in Latin. Daughter of Chronos and Rhea. Hera is Zeus's wife, and she shares in his royalty. Her symbols are poppies and pomegranates. The peacock is her favorite animal. She is a powerful and majestic goddess. She wears a long, pleated tunic over which she's draped in a large piece of wool cloth. She wears a crown on her knotted hair. She protects married women who are virtuous and faithful, and helps them during birth.

Hera did not take Zeus's infidelity well. The two argued often, and the sound of their voices boomed loudly in the sky. The goddess was jealous of her rivals, and every time she could, she would exact her cruel vengeance upon them. She even considered getting rid of her husband.

Unfortunately, Zeus wielded lightning—the most powerful weapon of all. He alone could use it to demand obedience. The gods had no choice but to listen. She felt it was excessive. She thought to dethrone him and take his place. And so, Hera began to plan.

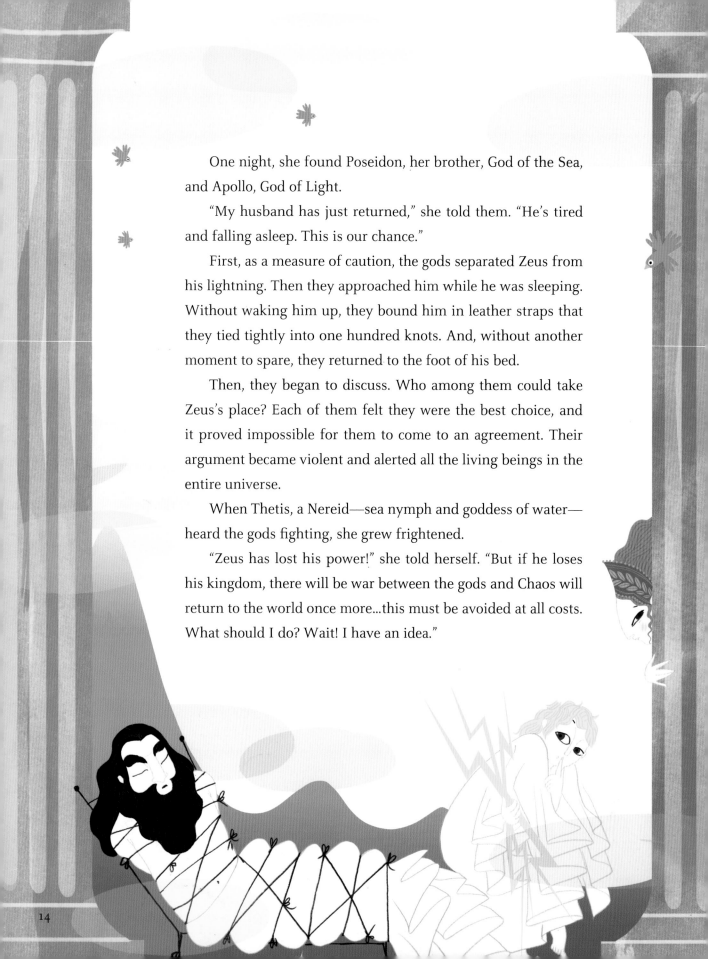

One night, she found Poseidon, her brother, God of the Sea, and Apollo, God of Light.

"My husband has just returned," she told them. "He's tired and falling asleep. This is our chance."

First, as a measure of caution, the gods separated Zeus from his lightning. Then they approached him while he was sleeping. Without waking him up, they bound him in leather straps that they tied tightly into one hundred knots. And, without another moment to spare, they returned to the foot of his bed.

Then, they began to discuss. Who among them could take Zeus's place? Each of them felt they were the best choice, and it proved impossible for them to come to an agreement. Their argument became violent and alerted all the living beings in the entire universe.

When Thetis, a Nereid—sea nymph and goddess of water— heard the gods fighting, she grew frightened.

"Zeus has lost his power!" she told herself. "But if he loses his kingdom, there will be war between the gods and Chaos will return to the world once more...this must be avoided at all costs. What should I do? Wait! I have an idea."

She made her way underground and descended all the way to Tartarus. There, she found Briareos, who guarded the door.

"Quickly, follow me!" she ordered. "I'll explain everything along the way."

With his hundred hands, Briareos easily undid the hundred knots that were holding Zeus. The god, finally awake, was overcome with rage.

Quickly, he punished the conspirators. First came Hera, since she was at the head of the conspiracy. He hung her by her wrists from the summit of Olympus, a heavy anvil hanging from each of her feet. She let loose a bloodcurdling cry, but nobody dared come to her aid. Then, Zeus sent Poseidon and Apollo to live among man. They were to help a king build the walls to what would later become Troy. Zeus decided not to punish the other gods who were only following the leaders. Now, he was certain his authority would never be questioned again.

When Zeus finally freed her, Hera returned to her palace, rubbing her wrists. Her favorite animal, the peacock, welcomed her, its feathers fanned out to her.

"What beautiful feathers!" she exclaimed. "But...there's something missing. Some light accents would make his blue look so much deeper...don't you agree?" she asked, believing Zeus to be by her side.

But Zeus wasn't there. He was on the ground, busy once more with his love for Io, the nymph. When he realized that his wife, still jealous, was looking for him, he quickly transformed Io into a cow.

But Hera wasn't tricked. She sent her servant Argus to make sure Io could not escape. Argus had one hundred eyes, and even when he slept, he always kept a few eyes open.

Zeus was worried. He asked Hermes, the cleverest of his children, to help him find a way out of trouble. The young god, disguised as a shepherd, approached Argus and, with his flute, managed to lull him to sleep. Then, he cut off his head.

Hera had seen everything from high on Olympus. In honor of Argus's good service, she collected his hundred eyes and used them to adorn the feathers of her favorite peacock.

That is why, when a peacock spreads its feathers, Argus's hundred eyes are said to open.

POSEIDON
God of the Sea

Neptune in Latin. Son of Chronos and Rhea. Poseidon is Zeus's brother. The oceans are his kingdom. His favorite animal is the horse. He is a quarrelsome and violent god, "He Who Shakes the Ground." He is a strong, bare-chested man with a trident in hand, ready to slam the seas, give birth to storms, or shake the ground, causing tsunamis and earthquakes.

Poseidon built his palace at the bottom of the sea. He rode around the world on a golden chariot pulled by four white horses, wearing bronze shoes, followed by a procession of dancing nymphs, the Nereids. The Tritons, creatures with the body of a man and the tail of a fish, also followed him, blowing in their conches to announce his presence.

When Poseidon wanted to marry, he began to court Amphitrite, a Nereid. But she hated Poseidon's violence, and so she ran away, taking refuge beside the Titan, Atlas. So, Poseidon sent her a dolphin to plead his case. The dolphin succeeded in convincing Amphitrite, and so she became his wife and queen of the seas.

But like his brother, Zeus, Poseidon was not a faithful husband. One day he met the Gorgons, three beautiful sisters, and fell deeply in love with one of them, Medusa.

"Come, follow me. Night is coming. Let us go to the shore to make love," he whispered in her ear. "I see a temple there; nobody will bother us there."

The temple belonged to none other than Athena herself. When she saw that the two lovers had the audacity to pass the night in her temple, she grew angry. Not daring to confront Poseidon directly, she transformed Medusa into a terrifying beast—golden wings, metal claws, long, sharp teeth, and serpent hair. From that point on, both gods and men ran from the terrible Gorgon, fearing her gleaming eyes, which would transform any who looked at her into stone.

One day, Perseus, a hero, avoided her petrifying gaze and succeeded in decapitating the Gorgon. The moment her monstrous head rolled in the pool of blood, a white winged horse sprang from the wound. It was Pegasus, Poseidon's son.

Newly born, Pegasus flew toward Olympus. He went to Zeus's palace where he was tamed by Athena, who then put him in the service of her favorite heroes, to help them defeat the monsters they faced.

Pegasus didn't dislike combat, but he did prefer the company of Muses. The nine Muses were Zeus's daughters, and they ruled over the arts, sciences, and literature. They liked to play, dance, sing, and make music on the wooded slopes of the mountains. Pegasus often joined them under the shade of these sacred forests, and, for their amusement, decided to slam his hooves on a rock. When he did, clear water sprang forth, and this spring became a place where poets would come for inspiration. That day, Poseidon was proud of his son, Pegasus.

DEMETER
Goddess of the Harvest

Ceres in Latin. Daughter of Chronos and Rhea. In her hands she often held a sheaf of wheat and a sickle. Her emblem is the poppy. Demeter is a tall, beautiful woman, tanned by the sun. A crown of wheat holds her blonde hair, and she wears a long, yellow dress, the color of the harvest. She teaches men how to farm. She protects the common folk, and, if properly worshipped, she grants them a bountiful harvest.

Demeter lived in Sicily, a rich, bountiful land for wheat to grow. There, she raised her cherished daughter, Persephone, far from the Olympians whom she didn't trust.

And then came Hades, with the sudden desire to get married. He said he needed a woman by his side to rule the Underworld. He thought of his beautiful niece, Persephone. She was young, sure, but what did it matter? Hades made his way to Olympus to get Zeus's approval. His brother gave it, but neither of the two thought to tell Demeter.

One beautiful spring morning, in a small valley, Persephone was picking narcissuses with her friends. They were competing to pick the biggest bouquet of flowers, and so she had walked away from her friends, hoping to find more flowers on her own.

Suddenly, a black chariot pulled by black horses appeared in front of her. Hades, who was driving the chariot, leaned forward and grabbed her. Persephone fought and cried, but the god of the Underworld held on to her tightly. He pulled her along as the ground opened and the chariot made its way down to the Underworld.

Everything happened so fast that nobody realized what had occurred. When Demeter learned that her daughter disappeared, her heart was filled with worry, and she set out, determined to find her. She covered Sicily, Greece, and even Asia. She looked for nine months, riding her dragon-pulled chariot, a torch lit with Mount Etna's flame in hand. In all this time she didn't drink, she didn't eat, and she didn't sleep.

One night, Zeus, moved by Demeter's anguish, forced her to swallow a drink made of poppy to make her fall asleep and allow her a reprieve from her sadness, even if only for a few hours.

Continuing her quest, Demeter at last arrived in Eleusis, in the south of Greece. She was received by its king and queen. When their eldest son returned from the fields, she questioned him.

"I may be able to give you a piece of useful information," he told her. "My brother was feeding his pigs when he saw the ground open in front of him and swallow one of his herd. It was then that he saw a chariot speeding along. It was pulled by black horses that made their way deep into the ground. He didn't have time to see the driver's face, but he did see that he was holding a woman in his arms, and he heard her scream..."

"Thank you, young man. The old goddess of the moon, Hecate, should be able to tell me more, since she sees everything when all else sleeps."

Hecate had heard the screams, but she didn't know anything else.

"Go to the Sun," she said. "He who brightens the world all day and knows all that transpires."

The Sun thought for a moment before he realized he had, in fact, seen Hades take Persephone.

"In my opinion," he added without a hint of malice, "Zeus must have known."

When Demeter heard his words, she grew furious.

"Ah! So, I have Zeus to blame for this! He must've taken great pleasure in my sorrow! If he thinks I'm going to throw myself at his feet, he is sorely mistaken. I won't give him the pleasure."

Demeter locked herself in her palace and remained there—neither speaking nor moving. She stopped providing her blessing upon the world, and as a result the harvests died. Seeds dried out, plants withered, and fruit spoiled. Crops died and there was nothing left to harvest. Men and animals alike were going to die of hunger, and still Demeter would not leave.

From the top of Olympus, Zeus was growing worried. He tried to reason with his sister—her daughter was happily married, and Hades was not a scornful type. He was the sovereign of the Underworld, and Persephone shared his throne. But Demeter wouldn't hear any of it, and the world, once lush and bountiful, continued to turn barren.

So, Zeus sent a messenger to Hades to let him know what was happening. He asked him to return Persephone to her mother. Hades accepted. He had realized that his young wife wasn't suited to the perpetual darkness of the Underworld and that she missed the light of day. But in order for her to return to the world of the living, she couldn't taste the food of the dead. Otherwise, she would not be allowed to leave the Underworld—that was the law.

But Persephone ignored that law. Not only did she eat pomegranate seeds, but she was seen eating them. When Demeter learned of this, she fell into despair once more.

Fortunately, Zeus found a compromise that Hades and Demeter both accepted. Persephone would spend six months of the year with her husband in the Underworld, and she would spend the other six months with her mother, becoming the symbol for the plants and crops which would sleep in the winter before being reborn in the springtime, in the light of the Sun.

ATHENA
Goddess of Honor, Wisdom, and Craft

Minerva in Latin. The daughter of Zeus and Metis. She wields a shield and spear. Her favorite tree is the olive tree, and the owl is her animal. She's a goddess with inscrutable, piercing blue eyes. They say she has an owl's eyes because she sees so clearly. She is Zeus's favorite daughter. She never married. Sometimes she goes by the name Pallas Athena, an homage to one of her childhood friends who died in an accident when they were young.

Zeus's first marriage was with Metis, the Oceanid he had met in Crete. Soon, she was pregnant with a child. Zeus was worried—what would happen if she gave birth to a boy as clever and cunning as she was? When he grew up, he would surely try to dethrone his father, like Zeus had dethroned Chronos, and like how, previously, Chronos dealt with Uranus.

The king of the gods had no intention of ceding his place to anyone. He had to stop Metis from giving birth to this child. And so, he needed to be more cunning than she was.

Since Metis was a shapeshifter, Zeus asked her to change forms, and so she shifted into a roaring lion. But would she be able to transform into a simple insect? Without suspicion, Metis transformed into a fly, and Zeus swallowed her.

Soon after, he was overcome with a terrible headache. In his despair, Zeus called for Hephaestus, god of the forge, and asked him for help. With one strike of his hammer, he split Zeus's head in two.

With a victory cry, Athena emerged from Zeus's head fully formed, wearing her helmet, armor, and wielding her spear and shield.

The goddess wielded her weapons in times of war. The leaders of armies would consult with her since she was a master of strategies and tactics. Unlike her brother, Ares, she held disdain for unnecessary violence and battles without honor. In times of peace, she would lay down her arms and wear a simple tunic instead. She taught man how to tame a horse, drive a chariot, and sail a boat. She taught women how to spin and weave wool. And it was from her that the city of Athens got its name.

Cecrops, the king of Athens, had built a town on a hill in the south of Greece. To choose its name, he called on the gods that lived in the region—Athena and Poseidon. The gods were jealous of each other and were unable to come to an agreement. So, Cecrops came to a decision—he would name the town after the god who offered the most useful gift to his people. The other Olympians would be the judges.

They met on the city's battlements. It was a hot day and the plains extended ahead of them, flooded by sunlight, without the least bit of shade. Poseidon made his way first, full of confidence, and slammed the ground with his trident. A horse emerged from the splintered ground.

"What a magnificent beast!" exclaimed the gods. "We could hitch him to a chariot when we go to war!"

Then Athena touched her spear to the ground, where an olive tree, full of olives, adorned with silver leaves, grew over the plains, providing a gentle shade.

"How pleasant!" said the goddesses. "The tree will shade us, and we could use the fruits! This tree represents peace."

Cecrops, who preferred peace to war, agreed with their opinion, and so Athena won, and the city became Athens.

ARES
God of War

Mars in Latin. Son of Zeus and Hera. His favorite animals are the rooster and the vulture. He looks like a fit, young man, wearing a helmet on his head and ready for battle.

Ares was born in Thrace, in the north of Greece—a country of oranges and wild horses where men dreamed only of war. Ares was handsome, but quarrelsome and ruthless. Zeus believed he had inherited Hera's worst qualities.

Like his sister, Athena, Ares was a master of war. But where the goddess fought honorably and for justice, the god relished his violence and bloodlust.

Ares never married, but he went on numerous adventures. Like many other gods, he fell in love with Aphrodite, the most beautiful of the goddesses and Hephaestus's wife. He had three sons with her: Deimos and Phobos, who fought beside him in the field of battle, and Eros, the god of love.

From their illicit romance, they also had a daughter, Harmonia, who was very different from her brothers. She was beautiful and gentle—practicing the arts and music most of all. It was thanks to her father's dragon that she met Cadmus, her future husband.

Cadmus was a Phoenician prince. He traveled the Mediterranean with his companions, searching all of Europe for his sister, who had been taken by Zeus. Guided by Athena, he arrived at the center of Greece. At the edge of the woods, he decided to stop to make a sacrifice to the goddess. To do so, he needed clean water. Since he could hear water nearby, he sent his companions to find some.

It turned out there was a source of water in the woods. It belonged to Ares and was guarded by a dragon.

Cadmus waited for his companions, but they didn't return. So, he left to search for them. He found only their bodies; the dragon had killed them all. At the moment, the animal stood in front of him at its full height, towering over the trees, breathing flames from its menacing face.

Cadmus didn't hesitate. There was a large rock at his feet. He winced as he picked it up and, with all his strength, he threw it at the dragon's head. The beast, surprised, was staggered by the blow and collapsed, dead.

Ares was furious. Not only did someone take his water without permission, but his dragon was dead. He brought the issue to his fellow Olympians, and, as a result, Cadmus was condemned to serve Ares for eight years.

At the end of his sentence, Athena gave Cadmus a gift— the region in the center of Greece where he would found the city of Thebes. While he was working in Ares's palace, he met Harmonia. They fell in love with each other. Finally free, Cadmus married Ares and Aphrodite's daughter.

Their wedding was lavish. The twelve Olympian gods attended, in twelve seats of gold specially built for them. Each gave a present to the young couple: Aphrodite, a golden necklace; Athena, a magic robe; and Hermes, a lyre for Harmonia to play her music with. Demeter promised them bountiful harvests, and the Muses sang and played the flute, led by Apollo.

Ares, forgetting his usual temper, was happy for his daughter.

APHRODITE
Goddess of Love and Beauty

Venus in Latin. Zeus's adopted daughter. Her sacred plants are the myrtle and the rose; her fruits, the apple and the pomegranate; her animals, the dove, sparrow, and swan. Destiny gave her the power to love and be loved, and to protect those who love each other. She often appears nude, covered only by her long, blonde hair.

Aphrodite was born from the foam of the sea. She rose from the water, naked, in a shell. Zephyr, the East Wind, pushed her along gently until she reached the island of Cyprus. There, she approached the shore. With each step she took, flowers and plants grew around her. The Seasons dressed her with jewelry and a magic belt that made all who approached her fall in love. The Graces followed her as she rode to Olympus in her chariot gently pulled along by doves.

One day, Aphrodite went to Thetis's wedding with Peleus. The gods had all been invited, even those of lesser importance. All of them, except Eris, goddess of discord, who pushed man and god alike toward strife, violence, and hate.

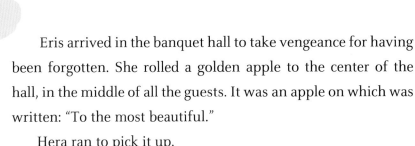

Eris arrived in the banquet hall to take vengeance for having been forgotten. She rolled a golden apple to the center of the hall, in the middle of all the guests. It was an apple on which was written: "To the most beautiful."

Hera ran to pick it up.

"It's mine," she said. "Am I not the queen of Olympus?"

"No!" cried Athena. "Why should it belong to you, rather than me? Am I not Zeus's daughter?"

"And what about me?" said Aphrodite with her soft, melodic voice. "I am the goddess of beauty. Everyone knows it."

Because the three goddesses were giving each other evil looks and seemed ready to break out into a fight, Zeus intervened.

"Now, now, ladies! Calm down...that is not for you or for us—the gods—to decide. We will give this to a mortal, Paris, the most beautiful of men, a prince who is, in fact, the son of the king of Troy. He keeps his beasts on the slopes of Mount Ida, not far from Troy. Hermes will bring you to him."

If Paris was surprised to see the three supreme goddesses arrive in front of him, he didn't show it. He accepted their offer to determine which among them was the most beautiful, by giving her the golden apple.

"But I'd like to see each of you alone, without your usual adornments," he clarified.

"Of course," said Hera and Athena simultaneously, removing their crown and helmet, respectively. "It wouldn't be fair if Aphrodite kept her magic belt, either."

And so they presented themselves, one after the other.

First Hera, majestic.

"If you choose me," she said, "I will give you glory and riches."

Then Athena.

"If you choose me, I will give you victory and wisdom."

"As for me," said Aphrodite, "I promise you only the love of the most beautiful woman in the world."

"Who is she?" asked Paris.

"Helen, wife of Menelaus, the king of Sparta."

"But she's married?"

"Who cares! As soon as she sees you, I'll make her so in love with you that she will follow you to the ends of the earth."

And so Paris gave the apple to Aphrodite.

The goddess of love held her promise. Paris, on a diplomatic mission to see Menelaus, stole Helen and brought her back to his home, Troy. Menelaus called all the leaders of Greece together to take vengeance on his honor, punish the people of Troy, and reclaim his wife.

And so began the war which lasted for ten years. While Athena and Hera came to the aide of the Greeks, Aphrodite protected the Trojans. But she couldn't prevent their defeat, nor the destruction of their city.

HEPHAESTUS
God of Fire and Forge

Vulcan in Latin. Son of Zeus and Hera. He wields a hammer and tongs, and the anvil is his emblem. Hephaestus, god of blacksmiths, wears a short worker's tunic and a round, pointy hat. He is bearded and smeared with soot. He walks with a limp, for which the other Olympians mock him. Despite their jibes, he is a clever and capable artisan.

Hephaestus was born lame, and so, upon his birth, Hera, his mother, got rid of him by throwing him out of Olympus. Fortunately, he fell into the ocean where Thetis and the other Nereids rescued him, but he retained his limp.

They brought him to Lemnos, a volcanic island, where they set up his first forge. He learned to work metals and make jewelry, which he offered to his benefactors. He also built weapons for the gods.

After nine years in their company, Hephaestus decided to return to his mother's side. Not without malice, he offered her a beautiful gift—a golden throne. Hera, delighted, sat on her throne. But when she wanted to get up, she found it impossible—she had been snared in her son's trap.

So, Dionysus, god of wine, went to Lemnos and offered his brother a drink so good that Hephaestus, well drunk, agreed to free Hera.

Sitting backward on the back of a donkey, Hephaestus made his way into Olympus. All the gods burst into laughter. Without dismounting, Hephaestus approached his mother and freed her. But before he did, he made her promise that she would help him get Aphrodite's hand in marriage. That was how the most reviled of the gods married the most beautiful of the goddesses.

They weren't a good match. Hephaestus spent all day working in his forge and when he returned home, covered in sweat and soot, he just wanted to sleep. With a husband like him, Aphrodite grew bored. She was often unfaithful, but Hephaestus, blinded by his love, didn't suspect a thing.

Aphrodite loved Ares, the handsome god of war and, every chance she had, she spent the night beside him. At dawn, they separated since they wished to avoid Apollo's jealous gaze, since he, too, loved Aphrodite. That's why Ares asked one of his servants to wake him up early, before the sun rose.

But one morning, Ares's servant forgot his orders, and so Ares continued to sleep. When the sun rose, Apollo was surprised to see Aphrodite and Ares together. He quickly told Hephaestus.

Immediately, Hephaestus set out to forge a massive bronze net, as fine as a spiderweb and so strong that nobody in the world could break it. He caught the adulterers, still asleep, and he called all the gods together so they could wake them up and shame them for their actions.

The goddesses, out of kindness, stayed home, but the gods were more than happy to oblige and watch the show. Aphrodite and Ares, finally awake, tried in vain to break the net that bound them.

"Oh my!" cried Hermes. "I wouldn't complain if I was in Ares's place, even under that net. King of the gods, what do you think?"

"I won't comment on a family affair," said Zeus.

"I understand," said Apollo.

They all began to laugh, but none among them pitied poor Hephaestus.

As soon as they were free, Aphrodite and Ares ran away—Aphrodite to Cyprus, her island, and Ares to Thrace. But before he left, Ares made sure to punish his negligent servant who didn't wake him, by transforming him into a rooster. Ever since that day, the rooster wakes up every morning at dawn to crow and signal the rise of the sun.

As for Hephaestus, he returned to his forge, far from the mocking Olympians, dedicating himself to making magnificent works.

HERMES
Messenger of the Gods; God of Wit, Commerce, Travelers, and Thieves

Mercury in Latin. Son of Zeus and Maia. His symbol is the caduceus, a staff entwined by two serpents, and surmounted by wings. In one hand, he wields a crook—the large staff used by both shepherds and travelers—and he wears a helmet and sandals, both adorned with wings. Messenger of the gods, he is also charged with taking mortals to the Underworld.

When Hermes was born in a cave in Arcadia, Hera was angry that she'd been once again deceived by her husband, and took it out on him and his mother, Maia. But the newborn Hermes rose to the top of Olympus, so thoroughly swaddled that the queen of the gods confused him with her own son, Ares, and offered him her milk. When she realized her mistake, she didn't have the heart to hate the baby she had nursed and decided to abandon her vengeance.

Hermes was a god full of both mischief and imagination. He was believed to be responsible for many inventions and, when he grew up, he often helped his father, Zeus, out of many tricky situations.

Hermes was still in his cradle, living with his mom in Arcadia. But as soon as his mother, Maia, turned her back, he would get up and leave to explore the world.

A few days after his birth, he went all the way to the north of Greece, where Apollo, his older brother, was grazing his herds. They were great specimens, just about to head back to their barns as night neared.

"They're beautiful!" thought Hermes. "I want them...but I can't get caught."

When night came, he led the cattle out backward so their tracks appeared as though they were headed toward the barn, even though he was leading them in the opposite direction.

When Apollo realized that his herd had disappeared, he grew angry and set out to search for the thief. He eventually came to Maia's cavern where Hermes was sleeping in his golden cradle, two cow skins serving as a rug.

"There he is! There's the thief!" he screamed as he pointed at Hermes. "That rug was one of my animals."

"That's ridiculous," said Maia. "How would a swaddled baby be able to steal from you? It's true that he's very clever. He just invented a new instrument, called a lyre. He took a tortoise shell, and for the strings, he used guts..."

"Cow guts! And where did he find these guts? You know that he's the thief!"

Apollo grabbed the laughing child and brought him to Olympus to stand before Zeus.

"My son can't be a thief," said the master of the gods.

But Hermes, after many questions, finally admitted it.

"I only killed two cows," he said, "to offer them in sacrifice to the twelve gods of Olympus."

"What twelve gods? We are only eleven..."

"I am the twelfth," said Hermes as he lowered his head.

Zeus began to laugh and asked his two sons to reconcile.

Together, Apollo and Hermes returned to the cave where the young thief had hidden the herd. As they were walking, he played the lyre, playing such beautiful sounds that Apollo said:

"Guard my herd, give me the lyre, and we'll be even."

Hermes accepted and, ever since that day, the lyre has been a symbol of Apollo, god of light, and now also the god of music.

ARTEMIS
Goddess of the Hunt and the Moon

Diana in Latin. Daughter of Zeus and Leto. Apollo's twin sister. The deer and wild boar are her sacred animals. Her hair is knotted and her dress is rolled up, held by a belt. Her legs are naked, and she wears light boots. She wears her quiver on her shoulder and holds her bow in hand. Her hunting dogs follow her, though sometimes she is also followed by a deer. A crescent moon rests on her head as her crown.

Zeus was in love with Leto, daughter of the Titans, and she was pregnant with twins. But when the jealous Hera learned of her, she asked Python, the serpent, to chase her to the ends of the Earth so none would welcome her. Leto was so distressed—she didn't know where she could go to give birth.

After crossing the Aegean Sea, she finally found refuge on the island of Delos. It was there that she gave birth to Artemis. Just born, she helped her mother give birth to her twin. Leto, lying between a palm tree and a date tree, suffered for nine days before giving birth to Apollo.

Her mother's suffering left such an impression on Artemis that she demanded Zeus allow her to never marry. All she wanted was a bow and quiver full of arrows, like her brother Apollo. She also asked for a retinue of nymphs who, like her, would never marry either. Zeus agreed.

Artemis made her home in the middle of the forests. Her chariot was pulled by white deer. At night, the nymphs would remove their yokes and brush them from head to hind. Then, they would bring them to drink from their golden troughs and feed from the meadows where Zeus's horses grazed.

Artemis loved to hunt. Though she would protect young animals, it was only to be able to hunt them when they were fully grown. She was not only caring, but also wild and indifferent, just like nature itself, and sometimes she was even cruel—as with Actaeon.

Actaeon was Apollo's grandson, but he was mortal. He loved to hunt and would do so whenever he had the chance. One such day, it was very hot, and so Actaeon turned to the young men following him and said:

"Let's stop. We've already killed many animals. The sun is scalding, and the ground is dry. Our dogs are as out of breath as we are. Let's rest, and tomorrow morning we will continue our hunt."

His companions agreed and took a seat at the edge of the woods. Actaeon himself wanted more shade, though. So, he followed a trail up, climbing over rocks, jumping over streams, happy to be on his own adventure in these unfamiliar woods.

Suddenly, he stopped. He heard the sound of splashing water and giggling women up ahead.

Curious, he continued forward. There, between the trees, he saw a group of girls playing in a lake of clear water. In the middle of them, standing taller than the others, was a stunning beauty. Some of the girls washed her with water, others rubbed her back, and some took care of brushing her wet hair. Actaeon was breathless as he watched them, too stunned to move.

Then, one of the girls saw him and cried out. They all turned toward him and surrounded the young woman in the center, to hide her from the stranger's gaze.

Slowly, the central girl turned to face the young man. She blushed, hesitated for a moment, and then threw water in his face as she said, "Now let's see who will listen to you when you say that you saw Artemis bathing!"

As the water splashed him, Actaeon felt himself transforming. His legs lengthened, his skin was covered in fur, and antlers grew from his head—he became a stag. In his new form he ran away, climbing over rocks, jumping over streams; his heart full of fear. Soon he heard barking: his own dogs had caught his scent; they were on his trail. Then, they caught up to him.

That was how Actaeon died for having seen what he shouldn't have—the goddess Artemis relaxing after her hunt, with her nymphs in a lake in the middle of the woods.

APOLLO
God of Light, Prophecy, Poetry, and Music; Patron of Herds and Flocks

His name in Latin is the same. He is the son of Zeus and Leto. Artemis's twin brother. His sacred symbols are the laurel wreath and, from among the animals, the dolphin and the swan. Apollo is handsome, blessed with eternal youth. He is often naked and without a beard, his blonde hair falling down his neck, adorned with a crown of laurels. But when he holds his lyre in hand, getting ready to play, he is dressed in a long tunic.

Not long after his birth, Apollo received a bow and set of arrows as a present. Immediately, he left for Delphi at the foot of Mount Parnassus. The hideous serpent, Python, who had chased his mother, Leto, when she was pregnant, was hiding there. To get revenge for his mother, Apollo pulled back his bow and, with a single arrow, killed the monster. Because he had the gift of prophecy, he settled down in Delphi and blessed the high priestess of his temple there with the ability to predict the future. He named her Pythia in memory of the serpent.

Apollo had a son, Asclepius. He was an excellent doctor, and his father was proud of him. Not only did he heal the sick, but he would even bring the dead back to life.

To Hades, the king of the Underworld, that was going too far! Seeing his subjects grow fewer, he complained to Zeus.

"What?!" exclaimed the king of the gods. "This young man is destroying the natural order of things. It is only normal that the dead give way to the living."

So he struck the insolent man down.

Immediately, Apollo, blinded by his pain and anger, took his revenge by killing the Cyclopes who had made Zeus's lightning.

Zeus couldn't tolerate such an act. He punished Apollo and banished him from Olympus. For one year, Apollo had to stay in Thessaly, in the north of Greece, where he would watch over the king Admetus's flocks.

Admetus treated the young god with much respect and goodwill, which Apollo returned in kind—all the females of his herds birthed twins, which doubled the size of the herd. As for the shepherds, Apollo taught them to play the flute, while he led them with his lyre.

After a year, Apollo, pardoned for his crime, returned to Olympus. But he did not forget the king of Thessaly, who had become his friend.

Admetus did not wait long before calling on Apollo. He had fallen madly in love with a beautiful princess from a neighboring kingdom, Alcestis. But her father would only give her away to someone who could yoke, on the same chariot, a lion and a wild boar, and then drive the two around a racing track.

"A man could never succeed in this," said Admetus. "But perhaps a god?"

So Apollo decided to help and succeeded in taming the beasts, which became very obedient. He assisted in Alcestis and Admetus's wedding and, as a gift, obtained Zeus's permission for a special favor. When the time came for death to take him, Admetus could be saved—someone else who loved him enough to die for him could take his place.

When Admetus died, his wife, still young, called for Apollo. But the immortal god could not take his friend's place.

To bring her husband back, Alcestis swallowed a poison and sent herself to the Underworld. Persephone, Hades's wife, greeted her.

"Your love for Admetus is admirable!" she cried. "But I don't think it's fair for a woman to die for her husband. Leave! Return to the world above, and enjoy the light of day together!"

And so, Admetus and Alcestis were reunited, and they continued to live together for many years, never forgetting to honor Apollo, to whom they owed their lives.

DIONYSUS
God of Wine, Vines, and Theatre

Bacchus in Latin. Son of Zeus and Semele. In one hand, he holds a thyrsus, a staff of giant fennel covered with vines of ivy, and in his other hand, a goblet of wine. His charriot is pulled by leopards. Dionysus looks like a very young man, almost an adolescent. A wreath of vines adorns his long hair. He wears a long tunic or a purple coat on his otherwise naked body.

Zeus, in the form of a simple mortal, seduced Semele, the princess of Thebes. She was already in the sixth month of her pregnancy when Hera found out. It didn't take long for the jealous goddess to find the young woman and, in the guise of her old nurse, trick her.

"My girl," she said, "what do you know of the man who pretends to love you? Maybe he's a monster in disguise? You should ask him to appear in his true form."

Semele, naive as she was, followed her advice. She begged Zeus so much that he finally relented, appearing in front of her in all his glory, lightning in hand. Semele's palace shot up in flames, and she died in the fire. But Hermes saved the child and placed it in Zeus's thigh, where it remained for the remaining three months before its birth.

To escape Hera's wrath, Dionysus hid with the nymphs of Mount Nysa in India. They pampered him and fed him honey. When he grew older, the muses taught him. They were often aided by Silenus, a cheerful old man who was often drunk, but wise and learned when he was sober.

Dionysus learned to make wine at the vineyards on slopes of Mount Nysa. Then he set out to conquer the world, conquering Egypt, Asia, and Europe.

During his travels, he was accompanied by Silenus, who rode a donkey, the Satyrs, men with feet like goats, and the Maenads—or Bacchantes—hedonistic nymphs who wore animal furs. They all sang and danced as they followed him playing their cymbals, flutes, and tambourines, encouraging all those they came across to join in their drunken fun.

Everywhere he went, Dionysus spread his cult and taught men to grow wine. Plays were put on in his honor, which is how he became known as the god of theater.

However, many refused to acknowledge Dionysus's godhood, and so he took cruel vengeance upon them. But he could also be kind and forgiving, as with the story of Midas.

One day, when the joyful band was traveling through Asia Minor, Silenus accidentally found himself lost.

After wandering for some time, he finally fell asleep in the gardens around Midas's royal palace.

The gardeners found him, in a deep sleep in the middle of a bed of roses. His donkey was grazing a short distance away. They woke him up, tied him up with a garland of flowers, and brought him to their master. With his round stomach, bald head, rosy cheeks, and his large red nose, Midas recognized Silenus. Happy to have met this jovial man, he decided to put on a grand feast that would last nine days and nights.

After the feast ended, he and his guards personally escorted Silenus back to Dionysus. The god of wine was sincerely thankful, having been worried about his old tutor's disappearance.

"How can I repay you?" he said to Midas. "Ask me for whatever you want."

"Well," said Midas, without hesitation, "I would like that everything I touch turn into gold. Then, I will become the richest man in the world."

The god was amused.

"If that's really what you want..."

Midas then touched a pine branch, which immediately turned to gold, gleaming like the sun. He stepped back, delighted. As he made his way home, the sand, pebbles, leaves, and flowers all transformed into gold that his guards could gather.

But when he made it back to his palace and he sat at his table, his chair, the tablecloth, and the dishes became gold, too, as did the drinks and the food that touched his lips. It didn't take long for Midas to grow hungry and thirsty—it was impossible for him to eat! Was he condemned to die?

He pleaded to Dionysus who, kindly, agreed to undo the boon he had placed on the king.

"If you want to get rid of it, go wash yourself in the Pactolus River," he said.

The king made haste and followed Dionysus's instructions, and ever since, flakes of gold have flowed down the Pactolus.

From then on, Midas turned away from his riches. He instead found pleasure in the forests around him and his garden of roses. Thanks to Dionysus, he had become wise.

Heroes and Gods

The gods possess powers that men and women don't have. They are immortal and can change forms as often as they like. But the feelings they experience are similar to those of mortals.

Heroes and heroines are men and women first; they tire, suffer, and die—they have the same qualities, the same faults, just to a greater degree. Though they're not quite divine, there is something superhuman in them—they are role models for us to learn from.

One characteristic all heroes share is a relationship with the gods, who either help or hinder them. Many of the heroes have divine origins—Achilles is Thetis's son and Helen is Zeus's daughter.

Why choose Jason, Theseus, and Achilles?

Jason is the first navigator—before Odysseus—to have set out on an important journey across the uncertain sea to wild and savage places. He didn't set out in the spirit of exploration or with a desire to conquer the world. Instead, he left on a quest for the Golden Fleece, which he needed to retake his rightful throne.

Theseus is a different kind of adventurer. He set out to slay monsters, like the famous Minotaur, to save lives and prove his courage. Afterward, he became a much-beloved king. He is even credited with bringing democracy to Athens.

As for Achilles, he was his best during war. He was a greater warrior, and despite his violence and bad attitude, he is one of the Greeks' most admired heroes.

But these heroes aren't adored only for their heroic qualities; they are also beloved for their faults and failings.

And the heroines?

Helen and Atalanta are worlds apart from the ideal Greek woman, who lives in the shadow of men, tending to her garden and rarely going out.

Helen left her home, husband, and son out of love for the man she ran away with. She also represents the danger of beauty—according to Priam, her face was that of a goddess, but thousands of men died in a war over her.

Atalanta is different. Shunned by her father and raised by hunters, she lived a life that intimidated men, developing equal athletic and hunting abilities, even though men would never recognize her talents. She is a great example of an independent woman.

JASON
The Argonaut

Jason was born in Thessaly, in the port of Iolcos. From the first day of his life, the ocean sang him to sleep, and he grew used to the rolling waves and the cries of seagulls. But because his uncle, Pelias, had stolen the throne from his father, the legitimate king, his mom thought it prudent to distance themselves. She feared for her son's life since he was the true heir to the kingdom. She trusted him to Chiron, a centaur, who lived in the forest on Mount Pelion.

Chiron wasn't like the other centaurs. Though he too was half-man, half-horse, they were loud and easily angered, whereas he was wise and learned. He taught Jason to respect nature, heal man and animal alike, and resist fatigue—a useful skill for his future adventure across the seas.

After several years, Jason decided to return to Iolcos and reclaim what was rightfully his. He left the forest, bidding his master goodbye, and came to a river. An old woman who was unable to cross was crying at the shore.

"Madam! Climb on my back, and I'll take you across the river!"

The old woman was heavier than he thought—she was actually Hera, the goddess, in disguise in order to test him. She and Athena wanted to know if Jason was worthy of the plans they had in mind for him.

When he arrived at Pelias's court, Jason was soaked to the bone, caked in mud, and missing a sandal he lost in the river—but he still looked proud.

Pelias looked at this young stranger and began to tremble—he had been told that a man, wearing only one sandal, would do him harm.

"Who are you, and what do you want?" he asked, his voice rough.

Without taking a knee, Jason told him.

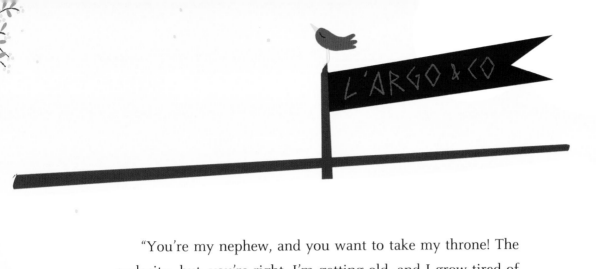

"You're my nephew, and you want to take my throne! The audacity...but, you're right, I'm getting old, and I grow tired of ruling. I am ready to hand over the kingdom but only on one condition: find me the Golden Fleece, which once belonged to our town of Iolcos. It is in the garden of the god of war, Ares, guarded by a dragon. It belongs to King Aeëtes of Colchis who is the son of Apollo. Surely you're not afraid of such a long journey to an unknown land at the feet of the Caucasus Mountains, near the Black Sea?"

"Afraid? Me? As soon as I find a ship, I'll go."

Jason had his friend Argo build a large ship for him—one that would be crewed by fifty rowers—and they named the ship the Argo, after its builder. The members of the team would be the Argonauts, and they had Athena watching over them.

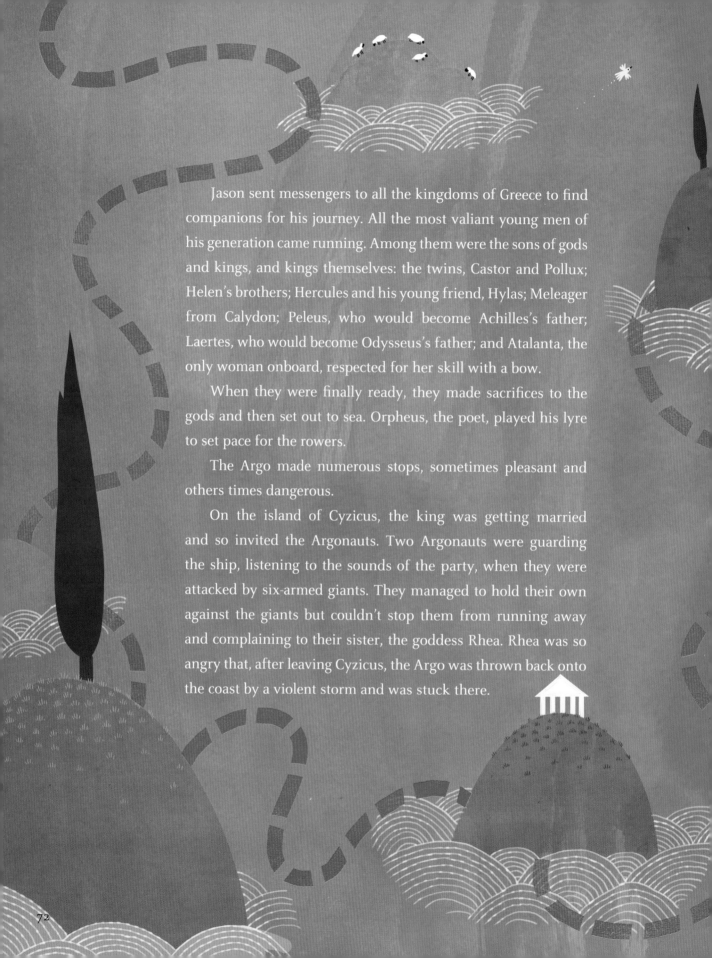

Jason sent messengers to all the kingdoms of Greece to find companions for his journey. All the most valiant young men of his generation came running. Among them were the sons of gods and kings, and kings themselves: the twins, Castor and Pollux; Helen's brothers; Hercules and his young friend, Hylas; Meleager from Calydon; Peleus, who would become Achilles's father; Laertes, who would become Odysseus's father; and Atalanta, the only woman onboard, respected for her skill with a bow.

When they were finally ready, they made sacrifices to the gods and then set out to sea. Orpheus, the poet, played his lyre to set pace for the rowers.

The Argo made numerous stops, sometimes pleasant and others times dangerous.

On the island of Cyzicus, the king was getting married and so invited the Argonauts. Two Argonauts were guarding the ship, listening to the sounds of the party, when they were attacked by six-armed giants. They managed to hold their own against the giants but couldn't stop them from running away and complaining to their sister, the goddess Rhea. Rhea was so angry that, after leaving Cyzicus, the Argo was thrown back onto the coast by a violent storm and was stuck there.

Taking advantage of a brief gap in the storm, a halcyon—a mythical bird said to be a sign of peace—flew down onto the bow of the ship and began to chirp.

"What is it saying?" Jason asked, turning to Mopsus, an Argonaut who could speak the language of birds.

"One moment...I'm listening...yes. The storm was sent by Rhea. She was angry that we hurt her brothers..."

"How can we make it up to her?"

"One moment...I'm listening. She says we should raise a statue for her and have a ceremony in her honor."

Argos took a piece of driftwood off the beach and sculpted a woman from it. The others planted it in the sand and danced around as Hercules gave them a rhythm to dance to with his mace.

Satisfied, the goddess granted them favorable winds. They reached the Sea of Marmara and stopped on another island to procure food and drink. The terrible King Amykos refused to supply them. Proud of his talent as a boxer, he challenged them, like he did with all strangers—a boxing match to the death.

"We're going to teach him a lesson," said Jason. "Pollux! You are Zeus's son and say you're the best boxer in the world. Prove it!"

Amykos was heavier than Pollux and wore gloves studded with iron, but Pollux was faster and, most importantly, more intelligent. He carefully studied his opponent before letting loose. As the fight wore on, Amykos was furious. His face bloodied and lips busted, he rushed at Pollux.

But Pollux dodged and struck back, breaking the bone in his temple. Amykos was dead, and the world was rid of another monster.

Next, they had to cross the Bosphorus strait. They stopped on the way to seek advice from Phineus, a blind seer, who told Jason, "If you hope to succeed, you must pray to the goddess of love, Aphrodite."

Then he explained how they could cross the Clashing Rocks.

"Two blue rocks stand at each end of the Bosphorus. They're barely visible in the fog and close in on any ship that tries to cross the strait. But if you set a dove free, it will rest on one of the rocks, and you'll be able to pass through unharmed."

The Argonauts followed his advice and, after reaching the Black Sea, continued on their quest. At this time, Hercules and Hylas set out on their own quest, leaving the Argonauts to continue without them.

Eventually, after many difficulties, they reached the mouth of a river. In the distance, they could make out a tall mountain range.

"The Caucasus!" cried Jason.

They had made it to Colchis.

They hid their boat in a cove and made their way toward the king's palace.

Aeëtes received them courteously, but when Jason revealed the reason why they had come so far, his attitude changed, and he declared, "You can take the Fleece if you can yoke two wild bulls to a chariot and plant a dragon's teeth in plowed soil— warriors will grow from them, and you will have to defeat them. What do you say?"

"I accept," said Jason. Though he didn't hesitate to reply, deep inside he was in despair.

Medea did her best to help. She was Aeëtes's daughter, the sun's granddaughter, priestess of the moon, and a magician. She was tall with black, wavy hair that fell to the floor. Due to Aphrodite's influence, she fell in love with Jason at first sight.

She was angry at her father for making such unreasonable demands. So, that night, she set out in secret, on her own, and followed the Argonauts back to their ship. She gave Jason an oil for him to cover himself with so he could better tame the bulls. She also gave him a magic rock and told him how to use it.

"I will save your life," she said. "I'm betraying my country and my father for your sake. In exchange, take me with you and swear you'll marry me."

Jason swore to all the gods that he would be her loyal husband for the rest of his life.

The trials were set to begin early the following morning in a vast, hilled field. The people of Colchis were there in great numbers, waiting for the show, while the Argonauts waited and worried.

First, they let the bulls loose. They stomped the ground with their bronze hooves and breathed fire. The crowd was screaming in both fear and excitement. Jason walked forward, brave and bold, and set his hand on the beasts' heads. They allowed themselves to be hitched to the chariot and worked for the rest of the day. That night, Jason planted the dragon's teeth. Armed warriors sprang forth from the ground, their weapons gleaming in the light of the setting sun. They were holding javelins, all pointed toward the Argonauts. The audience was breathless, standing, trying to get a better view. Medea trembled in fear and spoke a spell to protect the man she loved.

Free of any doubt, Jason threw the magic stone in the middle of the warriors. They turned to look at each other, surprised, and began to argue. It quickly escalated into battle and by the end, not one remained alive.

The Argonauts celebrated their victory and sought out their prize from Aeëtes. But the king was angry and refused to give up the Fleece.

Jason and Medea waited until late into the night before sneaking into Ares's garden. Medea used her magic to make the dragon fall asleep, and Jason grabbed the Fleece. They ran back to their ship, pulling up their anchor as soon as they got onboard.

When the Argonauts made it back to Iolcus, they expected congratulations. But they were disappointed—Jason's father had died, and Pelias, who had pushed Jason's father into despair, refused to give up his throne in exchange for the Golden Fleece.

Medea took vengeance for her husband. Using her magic, she killed Pelias. She and Jason were banished and took refuge in Corinth. They lived there quietly for ten years. They had two sons.

But where the Corinthians appreciated Jason for his strength, they feared the strange sorceress, Medea. She suffered for it and regretted leaving her country—she had abandoned everything to follow the man she still loved so passionately.

But he had grown tired of her. One day, Creon, the king of Corinth, suggested Jason send Medea home and, instead, marry his daughter, Creusa. He could keep his sons here with him and later inherit the kingdom.

Jason accepted.

Medea lost her husband, home, and sons—who would be treated as prisoners in Creon's palace. No! They'd be better off dead!

She arranged to have a beautiful wedding dress sent to Creusa. When the young woman received it, the dress burst into flames. The fire spread to the rest of the palace killing all those within. Jason managed to escape by jumping out of a window.

After having killed her sons, Medea took off, flying away on a chariot pulled by dragons.

As for Jason, he raised an army and conquered Iolcus, where he reigned for a long time.

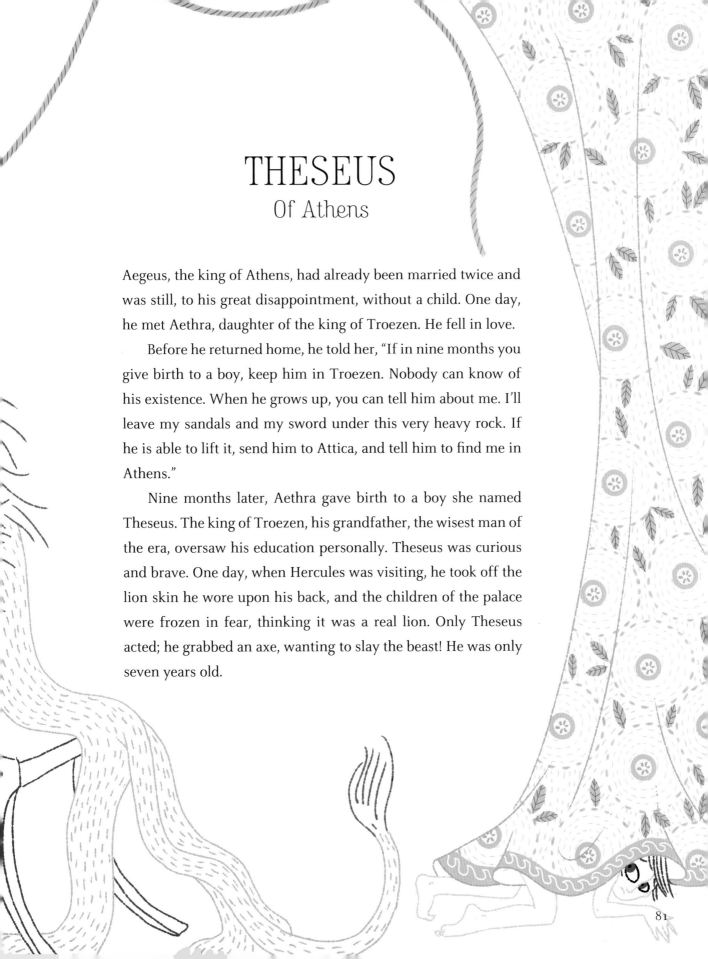

THESEUS
Of Athens

Aegeus, the king of Athens, had already been married twice and was still, to his great disappointment, without a child. One day, he met Aethra, daughter of the king of Troezen. He fell in love.

Before he returned home, he told her, "If in nine months you give birth to a boy, keep him in Troezen. Nobody can know of his existence. When he grows up, you can tell him about me. I'll leave my sandals and my sword under this very heavy rock. If he is able to lift it, send him to Attica, and tell him to find me in Athens."

Nine months later, Aethra gave birth to a boy she named Theseus. The king of Troezen, his grandfather, the wisest man of the era, oversaw his education personally. Theseus was curious and brave. One day, when Hercules was visiting, he took off the lion skin he wore upon his back, and the children of the palace were frozen in fear, thinking it was a real lion. Only Theseus acted; he grabbed an axe, wanting to slay the beast! He was only seven years old.

When he turned sixteen, Aethra told Theseus his father's name and brought him to the rock. He had a hard time lifting it but kept trying until he eventually succeeded. He put on the sandals and the sword and headed toward Attica. His grandfather recommended that he take a boat—the way was easier by sea than over land because of the many bandits. But Theseus wanted to know what he was capable of. Seeking to follow in Hercules's example, he was going to rid the region of wicked men.

The first bandit he met was killing travelers with a bronze mace. Theseus leaped forward, ripped the mace out of his hands, and caved his head in. He kept the weapon, confident it would be useful to him in the future.

Indeed, thanks to the mace, he overcame several bandits and even killed a giant boar so dangerous that the people in the area were afraid to leave their homes to farm.

But when he met Cercyon, who squeezed passersby to death with his giant arms, he didn't want to use the mace. Theseus had practiced wrestling since he was a child and challenged him to a match. He lifted the bandit by the knees and threw him on the ground, breaking his neck.

Finally, he met Procrustes, who owned a bed that could stretch or contract to different lengths. He invited travelers to rest in his bed. To some, he would offer a bed that was too short and cut off their feet so they would fit in it, whereas with others, he made the bed too big, and so he would stretch them out until he broke their bones. Theseus took the monster by surprise, laid him on the bed, and made him suffer in the same way he had with his victims.

When Theseus arrived in Athens, news of his exploits had already reached the city. He was welcomed as a hero.

But nobody knew he was the king's son.

Well, that wasn't entirely true...somebody had guessed it... Medea. When she had to flee from Corinth, she took refuge in Aegeus's court. They were married and had a child, Medos. But nobody knew that the king already had a son, Theseus.

But when she saw this young stranger who was dressed as a vagabond but still walked with a noble air, Medea knew who he was. Because of him, her son would not inherit the kingdom.

She led Aegeus to believe that the stranger was a dangerous spy and that it would be wise to poison him at the banquet that would be held in his honor. Though Aegeus hesitated at first, he was eventually convinced.

Theseus held the poisoned goblet in his hand when the roast was brought out. He set the goblet down and said, "As a child, I was taught how to cut meat. Please allow me to do so today."

He drew his sword and approached the roast. Aegeus recognized the sword—it was his own! His child was standing in front of him! He grabbed the goblet, spilled out the contents, and gave Medea a furious look.

She took Medos and fled the country, an exile once more. Aegeus let them leave and never saw them again. He had all his subjects recognize Theseus as his legitimate heir and threw a large festival in honor of the occasion.

The Athenians were happy, but some among them looked worried. Theseus wanted to know why.

A few years before, King Minos of Crete had sent his son, who wanted to see the world, to Athens. Unfortunately, while out hunting, his son died. Minos was furious and accused the Athenians of intentionally killing his son. To take vengeance, he deployed his fleet of warships on their coast. He won the battle and required Athens to send him a tribute every nine years— seven noble sons and daughters who would feed his Minotaur.

The Minotaur was a monster with the body of a man and the head of the bull. It was born from the love Minos made to a white cow. Minos wanted to hide the abomination from the eyes of the public, so he engaged the services of Daedalus, a renowned architect, and commissioned him to design a place to imprison the monster, which no one could escape once they entered. Daedalus created the labyrinth, a tangle of hallways, loops, intersections, and dead ends, where even he, after completing the work, had a hard time getting out.

And now the time had arrived in Athens once more. The young nobles had to leave for Crete on a ship with black sails—a sign of mourning. Theseus insisted to be sent with them so that he could kill the Minotaur.

"Do me a favor," his father asked. Take these white sails and hoist them when you return—that way I'll know that you've won.

"I will," said Theseus. "The gods are with me!"

Before leaving, he made sure to offer them sacrifices—to Apollo, who protects the young, and Aphrodite, goddess of love, who he favored above all others.

Aphrodite heard his prayers. When Theseus and the other nobles arrived in Crete, they were greeted by Minos and his two daughters. Aphrodite inspired the eldest daughter, Ariadne, to fall deeply in love with the young Greek.

He announced his intention to enter the labyrinth alone the following morning.

"No," thought Ariadne, "I won't allow this handsome young man to be devoured by that monster. I will do everything in my power to help him avoid such a gruesome death and help him escape that prison."

She went to find Daedalus to ask for his help.

She pretended that she had to enter the labyrinth and wanted to know how to escape it. Daedalus liked Ariadne, so he told her how.

"Minos destroyed the plans to the labyrinth. But I will explain how you can find your way. Take this ball of yarn and tie it to the door. Roll it out as you make your way through. In order to get out, you'll just have to follow the string in reverse."

Ariadne then made her way to the room where Theseus was resting.

"I can help you," she said, "but promise me first that you'll take me to Athens and marry me."

Theseus promised her everything she wanted.

So, she gave him the ball of yarn and explained how to use it. She added, "You shouldn't wait to challenge the Minotaur. At this time of the night, it'll be asleep. That will make it easier for you."

"But that would be cowardly!" said Theseus. "No, I'll fight him head-to-head, as honor dictates. I'll go tomorrow as planned. I promise to come back alive."

The following day, Theseus succeeded in killing the Minotaur, though it proved difficult. He saved the other nobles, who had been resigned to their fates. As soon as he exited the labyrinth, following the yarn that Ariadne had given him, they set sail and left Crete as fast as possible. It didn't take long for Minos to notice the disappearance of the Athenian nobles and his daughter. He sent a boat to chase after them, but the Athenians were too far.

During the journey home, Theseus thought to himself about his choices. Why did he promise Ariadne that he'd marry her? He was too young for marriage...and he wanted to meet other women...

When they made a stop on the island of Naxos to procure fruits and water, Ariadne fell asleep on the beach, and Theseus left her behind as he continued on his way back to Athens. He wasn't proud of himself. Fortunately for Ariadne, Dionysus, the god of wine, was passing through Naxos with his troupe of Satyrs and Maenads, dancing to the sounds of flutes and tambourines. He found the beautiful girl crying. He comforted her and married her.

Meanwhile, Theseus was getting close to the coast of Attica. He could imagine his father's joy, his relief at their return, and the people's cheering. He was so lost in his thoughts that he forgot to hoist the white sails like he promised.

Aegeus was watching from the top of the cliff. He saw the ship. The sails were black! His son was dead!

Filled with despair, he threw himself into the water.

Ever since, the Aegean Sea has held his name.

When he arrived in Athens, Theseus was both overwhelmed and triumphant. He seemed to have aged ten years. Because his father had died, he took charge of Athens.

He ruled wisely.

He changed the system of government—up until that point only kings held power. He proposed that the citizens of Athens form an assembly to make decisions and vote on laws together. He was content to command the army. That was how the world's first democracy was born.

Athens became a welcoming place for foreigners hoping to settle down.

The Panathenaic Games, held in honor of Athena, the city's patron, were opened not only to Athenians but to all of Attica's people.

Theseus was also the first king to mint currency, issuing coins depicting a bull in honor of his battle with the Minotaur.

Theseus went on many other adventures and traveled to many countries. He even went all the way to the Underworld, where Hercules would eventually rescue him. On his return to Athens, he left the city and died old.

HELEN
The Most Beautiful

Helen's birth was extraordinary. One day, King Tyndareus's wife, Leda, was walking on the shores of the river around the city of Sparta. She brought bread for the swans and one of the swans—the largest and most majestic of them—allowed her to pet him. In reality, the swan was Zeus in disguise.

Nine months later, Leda laid two eggs. In one was Pollux and Helen, Zeus's children; and in the other, Castor and Clytemnestra, Tyndareus's children.

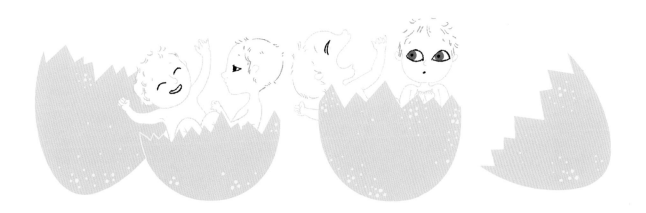

Helen was an exceptional beauty, even when she was little. When she was ten years old, Theseus and his friend, Pirithous, who wanted to get married, abducted her and drew lots for her. Theseus won. But she was too young to marry. So, he hid her with his mother, Aethra, in a village in Attica. He then followed Pirithous to the Underworld, to help his friend seduce Persephone, Hades's wife. Angered, Hades held the two of them as prisoners for many years.

During this time, Castor and Pollux freed their sister and brought her home to her adoptive father, Tyndareus.

When Helen was old enough to marry, all the young princes of Greece wanted her hand. Tyndareus was worried that Helen's choice would anger those who were turned away—it could result in civil war. He asked the wise Odysseus for his advice and did as he suggested, requiring all of Helen's potential suitors to swear that they would respect Helen's choice and serve her husband if she chose someone besides them. They all swore. So, Helen approached Menelaus and placed a crown of flowers on his head.

When Tyndareus died, Menelaus became the King of Sparta. He and Helen had a child together, a girl named Hermione, and they had a happy, easy life.

But the calm didn't last.

When Thetis, goddess of the sea, and Peleus, the mortal king of Thessaly, got married on Olympus, all the gods were invited—all save Eris, the goddess of discord. She, who loved arguments and conflicts, hatched a plan to get vengeance. On the banquet table, she placed a golden apple that read: "For the most beautiful." Immediately, Hera, Zeus's wife; Athena, his daughter; and Aphrodite, goddess of love, each tried to take the apple, saying that it obviously belonged to her. Zeus didn't want to offend any of them, and so he sent them to get a mortal opinion. That was how they came to Paris.

Paris was the son of Priam, the powerful king of Troy in Asia Minor. He ignored the promises Athena and Hera made him. Aphrodite offered him the love of the most beautiful woman in the world, Helen. And so, he gave the apple to the goddess of love.

Soon after, Paris went to Sparta on a diplomatic mission. With a group of Trojans behind him, they were received magnificently by Menelaus. During the banquets that followed, he confessed his love to Helen. She found the foreign prince handsome and was attracted by the riches he displayed. Pushed further by Aphrodite, she gave in to her passion and decided to escape her monotonous life. Menelaus didn't suspect a thing. When Menelaus had to leave for the funeral of one of his parents, Paris ran away with Helen. They got married at the first stop.

The Greek princes had sworn to support Menelaus against whoever did him wrong. They declared war on the Trojans and, under the command of Agamemnon, Menelaus's brother, prepared to set sail.

Paris and Helen didn't expect this when they arrived in Troy. It was a great city, with narrow streets, long avenues, temples, and palaces, looking over a vast plain that extended to the ocean. It was well-defended by thick walls and an army led by Hector, Paris's heroic brother.

In Paris's palace, Helen led a life very similar to her life in Sparta. She spun and wove wool, watched over the servants, received guests who traveled through, and when her husband went to battle, she helped him don the leopard skin he wore over his shoulders.

When Helen, Zeus's daughter, first arrived, the Trojans were blown away by her beauty. But when war threatened their city and required them to die because of her, their attitude changed, and they began to curse her name. Paris begged Hector and Priam, who respected the people, to swear they would protect Helen from any threats. They did.

One night, Helen, covered in a stunning white veil, followed by two servants, left the palace and walked along the ramparts, all the way to the Scaean Gates that led to the battlefield. The sun was setting, cicadas were singing, and the most noble of the old men in town were sitting there chatting. Because night was falling, the battle had stopped.

"Come here, my girl!" said Priam.

He turned to address his friends.

"We shouldn't be surprised if Trojans and Greeks fight for a woman like her! Her face is like that of a goddess...she is not to blame for her beauty, the gods are...but it would be better if she left so we could live in peace with our families."

The war had already gone on for nine years, sometimes favoring the Greeks, protected by Hera and Athena, and other times by the Trojans, aided by Aphrodite and Apollo. Zeus watched over the war. The best warriors in the world died, one after another.

In the tenth year of the war, Hector, who had been undefeated up until this point, fell to Achilles in battle. Paris took vengeance by shooting an arrow in the heel of the Greek hero, killing him. But Paris, too, would fall in time.

Helen was suffering. She couldn't stop thinking of all the men that were losing their lives because of her. She thought of Greece, of the children that were dying here in a foreign land, of the wives who would wait for their husbands in vain...she regretted leaving her country, her palace, her first husband, who had always been good to her and proved brave and skilled on the field of battle. She was sorry that she left Hermione, her young daughter.

One day she recognized Odysseus, disguised as a beggar, who had come to spy on the Trojans. She didn't expose him. Instead, she told him she knew who he was and secretly brought him to her palace where she offered him food and a bath.

When, near the end of the ten long years, the Trojans found an enormous wooden horse that the Greeks left them as an offering, to honor their gods and celebrate the end of the war, Helen guessed that Greek warriors were hiding inside. Though it spelled the end of Troy, she didn't a say word to anyone.

The two men she loved the most among the Trojans, Hector and Paris, were already dead. What did it matter to her if the city was destroyed? If Menelaus got his revenge and killed her? Destiny, which reigns over gods and men alike, would decide!

But when Menelaus found her in the rubble of the burning city, her clothes torn, face blackened by soot and covered in tears—but still beautiful—his heart softened.

He brought her back with him to Sparta, where she found her daughter and lived in peace for many more years.

ACHILLES
The Fearless

Achilles's parents were Thetis, an immortal nymph, and Peleus, king of the Myrmidons in Thessaly. They were proud to have such a beautiful baby.

The Nereid wanted her son to be immortal like her. She brought him to the edge of the Styx, the river that separates the world of the dead from that of the living and makes those who bathe in its waters invincible. She dipped her son into the river, headfirst, holding him by the foot. From that point on, no injury could kill him except on his heel, which she had used to hold him. Achilles's heel would remain his weakness.

Achilles grew up. Everyone admired his golden locks, his confidence, and his speed—he was faster than a deer being chased by dogs. He was as capable of violence as he was generosity and tenderness. He wasn't afraid of anything or anyone.

His parents entrusted his education to the centaur, Chiron, who had raised Jason. Chiron quickly understood that Achilles would be a warrior and that he'd rather fight for glory on the fields of battle than deal with the worries of an easy life. To strengthen the child, Chiron fed him the flesh of lions and the bone marrow of bears. He taught him how to ride a horse, hunt, treat wounds, and play music. Patroclus, his cousin, was his companion in all things—both studies and games. They were inseparable.

When war broke out in Troy, Achilles, fifteen at the time, had yet to even grow a beard. Thetis knew that if her son left for battle with the Greek kings he would die at Troy's Scaean Gates. She dressed him in women's clothes and, under the name Pyrrha, entrusted the king of Skyros—a small island on the Aegean Sea—to hide her son amongst his daughters.

Achilles stayed there until the day Odysseus, charged by the rest of the Greeks with finding the young warrior, came with a large basket, filled with presents for the girls: belts, scarves, jewelry. Then a trumpet sounded outside, and all the ladies ran away.

"We're under attack!" they screamed.

Suddenly, one of the ladies took the sword at the bottom of the basket and ran toward the door—Achilles had revealed himself!

He returned to Thessaly and asked his father for fifty ships to join the Greek fleet, commanded by Agamemnon. Along with his Myrmidons, he also brought two immortal horses as fast as the wind that Zeus gifted to Peleus to tie to his chariot, and an ashen spear so heavy only he could wield it.

After a long and difficult journey, the Greeks made it to Asia. They dropped their anchors and built a base on the beach, erecting a wooden palisade and a ditch to protect it. Ahead of them, the Scamander river, with its swirling waters, flowed along the plains and, further in the distance, up on a hill, was the city of Troy.

The war dragged on for ten years. The war ebbed and flowed, the advantage shifting from the Greeks, aided by Hera and Athena, and the Trojans, backed by Aphrodite and Apollo, and back again. While waiting for a decisive battle, the Greeks explored the region and took the riches and women they found. Then they shared them with each other. Agamemnon, the leader of the Greek forces, gave himself the best share.

For his share, Achilles received Briseis, a beautiful prisoner who he fell in love with, while Agamemnon took Chryseis, the daughter of one of Apollo's priests. The god, angered that someone had dared to take the daughter of a priest from his temple, spread pests around the Greek camp. To appease him, Agamemnon had to return the young woman to her father. But he then demanded compensation from his allies.

Achilles chided him for being too demanding, angering Agamemnon.

"If that's what you think, then I'll take your prisoner, Achilles! Briseis will replace what I've lost."

Achilles didn't reply, but inside he was furious. He decided to let the Greeks continue the war without him. He went into his barracks with his cousin Patroclus and their soldiers.

It wasn't easy for him because he loved battle. As for the Greeks, they had it even harder because they lost their strongest warrior, not to mention that their prophets had predicted that they couldn't win the war without him. As a result, Hector led the Trojans all the way to the Greek camp. They leapt over the ditch and began to break open the palisade. They were preparing to burn down the boats.

Ajax the Great, a respected Greek warrior, and Odysseus went to visit Achilles together and request his help. They found him sitting outside his shelter, playing his lyre and singing to pass the time. Patroclus was enchanted as he listened. Achilles received the two messengers politely but refused to change his decision. But the next morning, Patroclus was worried about the enemy's advance. Achilles allowed him to take his armor and horses for his chariot. He then asked the Myrmidons to follow their new leader's orders.

In his fervor, Patroclus succeeded in pushing the Trojans all the way back to the walls of their city. He killed many but was finally killed in turn by Hector, who stripped him of his armor—Achilles's superb armor—and took it as a trophy he stored inside Troy.

Though it was hard, the Myrmidons managed to bring Patroclus's body back to camp. They were all crying—even the immortal horses shed tears—because Patroclus was a kind man and a good warrior. Achilles, deep in despair, pulled out his hair. He hated himself for having let Patroclus go to battle without him.

Thetis heard his cries. She ran to her son's side.

"I will take vengeance for Patroclus!" he cried. "But how? I have no armor or shield."

"I'll take care of it," said the Nereid.

She went to the workshop of the god of the forge, Hephaestus. When he saw Thetis, he cleaned his face, which was covered in soot and sweat, and limped toward her. He was being helped by beautiful, golden women—automatons he had built in his forge.

For Thetis's son, he quickly made a gleaming set of armor: a breastplate, greaves, a helmet with golden plumes, and a large shield reinforced with five bronze plates and beautifully decorated.

As soon as Achilles donned his new armor, he grabbed his lance and jumped onto his chariot, the Greek troops following behind him. Rage and despair drove him forward. The Trojans recognized him from afar. He was shaking. In the meantime, led by Hector, the Trojans advanced. The charge was devastating. Many died. In the heat of the action, Achilles was ruthless. He took twelve young Trojan nobles hostage to sacrifice on Patroclus's pyre.

Soon, the plain was no longer enough for him. He fought in the Scamander river, which pulled the bodies of the fallen men and horses into its whirlpool. When its bed was full of bodies, the river—which was also a god—grew angry, left the river, and chased Achilles, who was responsible for the massacre.

Achilles ran away. Despite his speed, he was almost caught. But how could he, who was invincible, die of drowning, with no glory to be had? He begged Zeus, who sent his son Hephaestus to use his fire to stop the overflowing waters. Achilles was breathless, but he was safe. Night came, and each side returned to their camp.

The Greeks congratulated Achilles, who gave them a chance to rest. But he wasn't satisfied. He wanted to fight Hector—the man who had killed Patroclus—in single combat and test Hector's reputation as the greatest warrior of his time—after Achilles himself, of course.

The following morning, the two armies were frozen as they watched the duel. First Hector ran around the city three times as Achilles chased him. As he started to gain distance, the Trojan finally turned to face him. They fought bravely and valiantly—they were equal in strength. But Athena intervened and tricked Hector—giving Achilles the chance he needed to kill the leader of the Trojan army.

Before he died, he asked his rival to let his parents take his body so they could perform his funeral rites.

"No!" cried Achilles. "Don't count on it. You've hurt me too much. I'll be feeding your body to the dogs!"

"You're ironhearted! Watch out...the gods...at the Scaean Gates..." murmured Hector before he died.

Achilles removed Hector's breastplate and pierced his heels to pass a rope through, and attached Hector to his chariot, which he sent into a gallop across the plains. The hero's body bounced against the ground as his hair swept the dust. From the top of the ramparts of the city, Priam, Hecuba—Priam's wife and Hector's mother—and all the people of Troy watched, tears streaming down their faces.

The following day, during a truce, Achilles built a massive pyre for Patroclus and he dragged Hector's body around it three times. Then, as custom dictated, he organized funeral games: chariot races, boxing, wrestling, foot races, javelin tosses, and archery competitions.

The battle had yet to pick up again. One night, after dinner, Achilles heard a chariot. An old man stepped down from it, walked over to him, and fell to his knees, kissing his hand. It was Priam, the king of Troy, who had come to reclaim his son's body. As ransom, he brought a chariot full of treasures.

"Respect the gods, Achilles," he said uncertainly. "In your father, Peleus's, honor, take pity on me. He can wait for your return in his country. But I can't, because Hector will never return. And I had the courage to do what no man would, I kissed the hand of his murderer."

Achilles was moved. He gently pushed back the old man and invited him to sit. Each thought of what they had lost. One, his best friend, the other, his son. What's more, Achilles knew he would never see his father again, because his destiny was to die under the walls of Troy.

He accepted the ransom Priam brought and asked his servants to wash Hector's body away from them, so that Priam would not see the state his son was in. Achilles gave Priam a jacket and proposed a twelve-day truce, to allow the Trojans to organize a funeral. He admired the old man's courage and his dignity when he spoke. Priam, on his end, also admired Achilles, who was tall, handsome, and, in many ways, like a god.

The old king left in the night with his son's body.

When the truce ended, the fighting continued. This time, Paris, Hector's brother, was aided by Apollo and shot Achilles in the heel with an arrow.

Achilles died at the feet of the Scaean Gates, as was foretold.

But he remained in the minds of men as one of the most celebrated heroes of antiquity.

ATALANTA
The Light-Footed

When Atalanta was born, her father, Iasus, the king of Arcadia, was angry. He wanted a son who could become a warrior or a famous hunter and inherit all that was his. But he had a daughter! As was the custom in those times when one didn't want to keep their child, he brought the baby to the wooded slopes of a mountain, near the city of Calydon, and abandoned the little girl.

Artemis, goddess of the hunt, happened to be nearby at the time. She heard a newborn crying and found a beautiful, healthy little girl who demanded to be fed. At this time, bears lived in the forests and were among Artemis's favorite animals. She asked one of the bears to nurse the child and entrusted her to a group of hunters. They raised her and taught her all they knew—how to live in nature, the habits of wild beasts, how to shoot a bow, throw a javelin, and use a cutlass. By the time she was an adolescent, Atalanta was already a more capable hunter than many men. And because she was so fast in foot races, she was given the nickname "Atalanta the Light-Footed."

When Jason set out to capture the Golden Fleece, he gathered all the most valorous young people in Greece. Atalanta was the only woman among them. Some of their party protested—she was too pretty to risk in the danger ahead...she should stay home to spin and weave wool...but Jason knew her reputation. And so, she stayed on board the Argo to take part in the hunt.

After several years, Atalanta returned to Greece, hoping to find her family and gain her father's respect. Iasus must have known that she was one of the Argonauts, but for some reason he didn't receive her.

She then heard of a particularly dangerous boar hunt that was happening in the forests of Calydon. She had to take part, no matter what! Maybe in doing so she'd finally be able to reach her father's heart?

What had happened was that the king of Calydon, Oineus, had angered Artemis when he offered sacrifice to the twelve gods of Olympus and forgot the goddess of the hunt. She took revenge by sending a monstrous boar to attack the king's men and ravage his crops.

Oineus called all the most valiant men in Greece, including Jason; Theseus of Athens, and his friend Pirithous; Castor and Pollux, Helen's twin brothers; Peleus, who would become Achilles's father, and his brother Telamon, who were Oineus's brothers-in-law; as well as his own son, Meleager.

Atalanta also presented herself.

When Meleager saw this slender, young woman, who moved so gracefully and stood tall with such confidence, Meleager fell in love.

"Whoever marries her will be a happy man!" he said, making the men of the group, and his uncles in particular, uncomfortable.

"A woman! She can only bring us bad luck!" they complained.

They demanded that she be placed at the back of their group, far away from them.

Under the moonlight, they made their way deep into the forest. Some of them were armed with lances, javelins, and axes, and others—including Atalanta—wielded bows. They walked forward in silence, a few feet away from each other, toward a glade of willow trees near water where they found the boar.

The animal was swimming. It heard them, jumped out of the water, killed two of the hunters and injured another, and a fourth hunter quickly climbed up a tree. Peleus and Telamon courageously approached the boar, lances in hand. But Telamon's foot got caught in a root and he fell. As Peleus was helping him stand, the boar charged them. That would've been the end of them if Atalanta hadn't been able to fire an arrow and hit the beast behind the ear, sending it running, temporarily.

Behind her, Ancaeus said, "That's no way to hunt! Watch and learn!"

He threw his axe at the boar and missed. The animal turned around, charged, and disembowled him.

Then it was Theseus's turn, but his javelin missed, too. Fortunately, Meleager had his own javelin in hand, and he reached the boar's right side as it was turning toward him, trying to get the arrow out of its injury. That gave the young man the chance to stab his lance into the monster's flank all the way to its heart. With that, the monster died.

Meleager skinned the beast and offered it to Atalanta as her just reward, saying, "You made the boar bleed first, and if he hadn't died from our attack, your arrows would've finished it."

But Meleager's uncles were furious that he would dare give the honor to a woman. If their nephew didn't want it for himself, he should've offered it to his elders: them.

Meleager, still full of adrenaline from the hunt, grew angry, and as his anger festered, he ended up killing his uncles.

A civil war followed, during which Meleager died.

In the meantime, Iasus finally recognized his daughter's bravery. He welcomed her warmly and announced that she should marry in order to make sure to have an heir. But she didn't want any part of it.

Atalanta was used to living alone, except for the dangerous expeditions she went on, and she enjoyed her life. She had never been in love and couldn't imagine submitting to a man. In addition, Apollo's priestess at Delphi had predicted that if she took a husband, great harm would to come her.

Atalanta the Light-Footed knew that nobody could beat her in a race. Because her father insisted, she said she would accept marriage if he organized a competition—she would marry any suitor who could beat her in a race. If they couldn't win, they'd be put to death. With those conditions she hoped that none would try for her hand. But she was disappointed.

Despite the penalty of death, there were many young men who were lured to Iasus's court by Atalanta's reputation. They were all defeated, but more always came.

"I don't understand," thought Hippomenes, who came from Arcadia to assist in one of the races. "Lose your life to win a woman...I can't imagine it's worth the risk!"

But when he saw the young woman arrive in the stadium, he changed his mind.

Her short tunic showed off her athletic body, the wind made her hair float in the air and caused the ribbons on her sandals to flutter. Her pale complexion flushed with the effort of running. She was so beautiful!

She won the race easily, and the losers suffered their fate.

"I understand the suitors now," thought Hippomenes. But these men were worthless...I'm better than them. Why don't I give it a try? May the gods help me!"

He found Atalanta to congratulate her and tell her that he wanted to compete.

"If I win, you won't be embarrassed to marry me. My father is a king in Boeotia and the god of the sea, Poseidon, is among my ancestors."

Surprised, Atalanta looked at him. He was handsome! And young...almost a boy! How brave! It would be too bad if he died.

She tried to make him change his mind, but he refused.

For the first time the young woman was worried about one of her suitors. She almost wished she would lose to save his life.

Hippomenes was confident, but he judged it prudent to ask Aphrodite for help. Goddess of love, she would surely come to his aid.

Aphrodite was on her island, Cyprus. As she walked around her orchard, she had grown three golden apples. She gave them to the young man and told him how to use them.

When the race began, the stadium was full. From the start of the race, the spectators favored Hippomenes. They felt he would win because of his youth, good looks, and clear complexion, and they screamed in support.

"Go for it! Don't be intimidated!"

Atalanta seemed to fly. For a while they were each as fast as the other. And for a moment Hippomenes even broke ahead from Atalanta. The crowd cheered and cheered.

But a few minutes later, he began to tire. His mouth was dry, and he was out of breath. So, he took the first golden apple from his tunic and sent it rolling down the track. Surprised, Atalanta bent down to pick it up, giving Hippomenes a chance to recover his breath and run past her.

But his lead was short-lived. He then dropped the second apple, which the young woman picked up once more, and he passed her again. But she wasn't angry. Though she felt a desire to win, she also hoped to spare him from the horrible fate that awaited him—for the first time, she regretted the cruel rules she had set.

Hippomenes, encouraged by the crowd, was gaining a lead. But he began to run out of breath again. He was so close to the finish line; it would be too bad. He sent a quick prayer to Aphrodite and, with all his strength, threw the third apple on the side, as far as possible. Atalanta hesitated for a moment—if she went to grab it, she risked losing the race, but the shining, golden fruit was irresistible. She gave in to the temptation and Hippomenes won the race.

They married each other. In his joy, Hippomenes forgot to thank the gooddess who made it possible for him to win Atalanta.

Aphrodite decided to punish them.

One night, while the two were traveling, they entered a temple to spend the night. The temple was dedicated to Rhea, mother of the gods. Their presence desecrated the sacred space. Aphrodite told Rhea and she transformed them into lions that she hitched to her chariot.

Atalanta, as a lioness, had kept her soul. She wanted to know why she, who hadn't asked Aphrodite for anything, had been punished this way. Should she have been wary of love and kept her independence? She longed to once again run free.

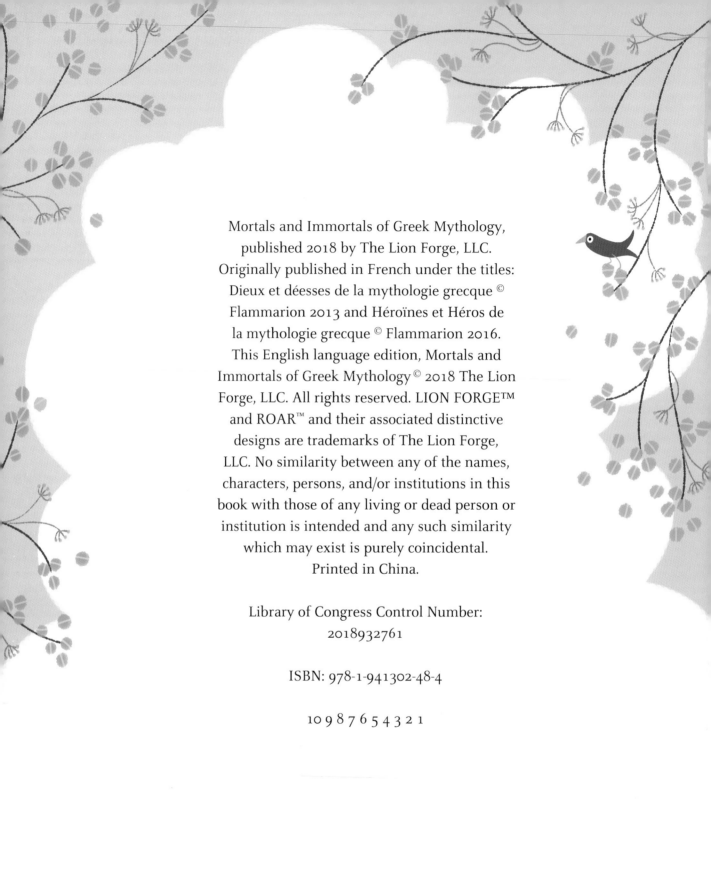

Mortals and Immortals of Greek Mythology,
published 2018 by The Lion Forge, LLC.
Originally published in French under the titles:
Dieux et déesses de la mythologie grecque ©
Flammarion 2013 and Héroïnes et Héros de
la mythologie grecque © Flammarion 2016.
This English language edition, Mortals and
Immortals of Greek Mythology © 2018 The Lion
Forge, LLC. All rights reserved. LION FORGE™
and ROAR™ and their associated distinctive
designs are trademarks of The Lion Forge,
LLC. No similarity between any of the names,
characters, persons, and/or institutions in this
book with those of any living or dead person or
institution is intended and any such similarity
which may exist is purely coincidental.
Printed in China.

Library of Congress Control Number:
2018932761

ISBN: 978-1-941302-48-4

10 9 8 7 6 5 4 3 2 1